My Daddy Is a Pretzel

Yoga for Parents and Kids

"I am a teacher. A teacher is someone who leads.
There is no magic here. I do not walk on water.
I do not part the sea. I just love children"
— Marva Collins

For Luke, Jacob and Malachi,
the astronauts of the family
— B. B.

To my dear friend
Sophie and Mrs. Pilou!
— S. F.

Barefoot Books
2067 Massachusetts Ave
Cambridge, MA 02140

Text copyright © 2004 by Baron Baptiste
Illustrations copyright © 2004 by Sophie Fatus
The moral rights of Baron Baptiste and
Sophie Fatus have been asserted

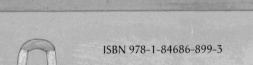

Barefoot Books
29/30 Fitzroy Square
London, W1T 6LQ

First published in the United States of America
by Barefoot Books, Inc in 2004
This paperback edition first published in 2017

ISBN 978-1-84686-899-3

British Cataloguing-in-Publication Data:
a catalogue record for this book is available
from the British Library

Library of Congress
Cataloging-in-Publication Data
is available under
LCCN 2004004655

Graphic design by Katie Pringle, Bristol, England
Photograph of Baron Baptiste by Tara Sylvester
of Mountain High Portraits
Reproduction by Bright Arts, Singapore
Printed in China on 100% acid-free paper
This book was typeset in Christiana Regular, Galahad
and Kidprint
The illustrations were prepared in acrylics and pastels

3 5 7 9 8 6 4 2

My Daddy Is a Pretzel

Yoga for Parents and Kids

BARON BAPTISTE

with illustrations by Sophie Fatus

Barefoot Books
Step inside a story

Introduction

When I was a boy, the adults in my life helped me to find figures who possessed qualities worth striving for: athletes and explorers with exceptional powers of perseverance and self-discipline; martial artists who had mastered both body and mind; politicians and other agents of social change who dared to face the unknown, standing up for what deserved to be loved and protected; and spiritual leaders who possessed the traits of character we most admire: honesty, compassion and courage. As I grew older, I learned that noble people (heroes) could be found closer to home too — among my friends and family members . . . in fact my own parents were courageous pioneers in helping to establish yoga in America.

Looking back, I see how lucky I was that my parents and so many of my teachers thought it was worthwhile to pursue yoga, to meditate and to pay attention to their physical and spiritual health. Their commitment gave me a "picture" of what vitality and virtue looked like and showed me how I could apply these ideals to my own life. Now, as a parent in turn, I set out to pass these same ideals down to my three sons, sharing yoga with them and encouraging them to do their best and achieve their potential. With this book, I hope to help you too. The practices here give children and adults alike targets to aim for and examples to follow, while the storyline shows how the benefits and inner meanings of the yoga postures relate to the way we live, whatever our profession or status in life.

As every parent understands, children imitate what they see, hear and feel. They naturally look for examples to follow. Although children have an inner compass that points them towards a true north, they do not know the difference between habits that give life and habits that take life away. They simply imitate and do what they see, hear and experience. So it makes a big difference when we adults make efforts to give direction and show what habits lead to a vital, healthy and happy life.

In this book, I set out to share with you the time-tested task of training the hearts, minds and bodies of the young. This task involves explicit training in good habits, and it involves the example of adults who, through their daily routine, show children that they take spiritual virtue and physical vitality seriously — but not without losing their sense of fun! The message and the activities in these pages will help children to enjoy the benefits and rewards of yoga practice. It is never too early to start. These postures and the philosophy behind them have the power to impress themselves upon young minds and to remain as lifelong guides, as tools for practice and signposts that point the way.

My goal is to present health and virtue not as something to possess or to have, but as something to be — as the most important thing to be. As we read this story to our children and share the postures, we begin to acquaint them with the idea that the life of good health, and the life of virtue and vitality, is worth living. We invite them to lift their young eyes, to reach up and to grow into brave and powerful young people. For it is by striving for the best in ourselves that we empower our children and show them that they too can live with the nobility of heroes.

BARON BAPTISTE

Today, in class, we're going to say
What jobs our parents do each day.

Niki says her mother's a gardener.

Sometimes, my daddy's a tree.

The Tree Pose

Vrksasana

The tree pose teaches us to support ourselves with strong roots, so that we can reach high and remain stable, yet be flexible, at the same time.

1 Stand straight with your feet below your hips.

2 Inhale and lift your right foot up to your inner thigh.

3 Bring your hands together at your heart.

4 Sweep your arms up above your head.

5 Interlace your fingers, palms up, and stretch tall.

6 When you are ready, lower your arms and your right foot as you exhale.

Lionel says his parents are vets.

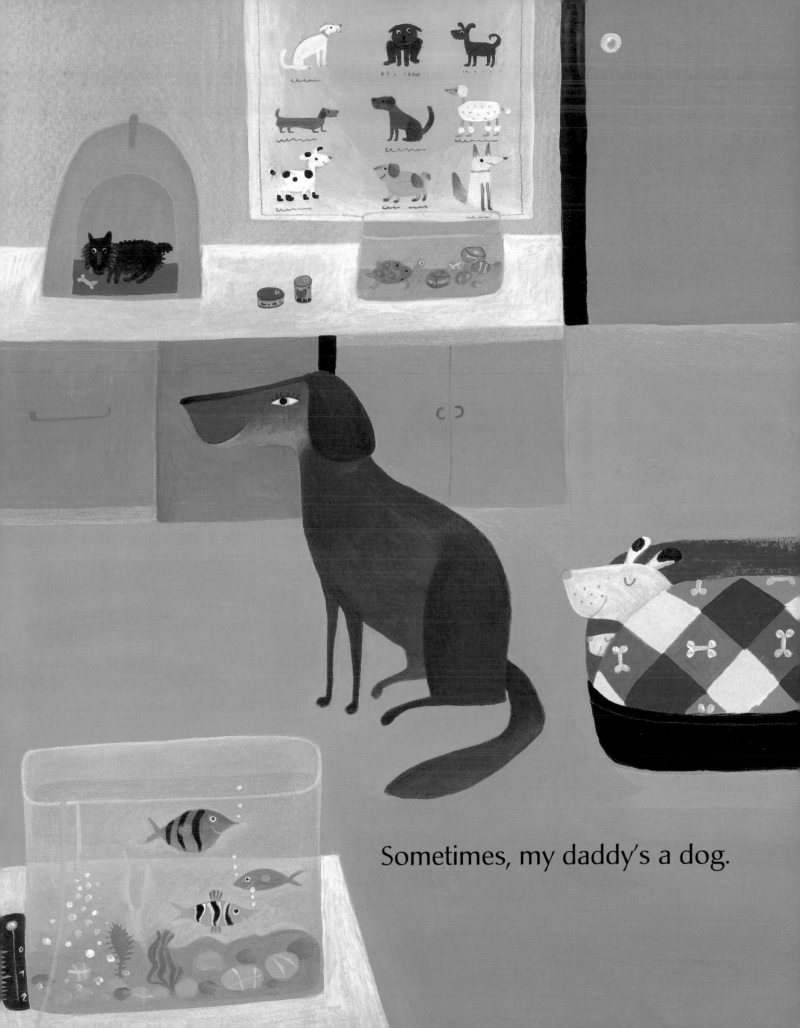

Sometimes, my daddy's a dog.

The Dog Pose
Adho Mukha Svanasana

Have you noticed how supple dogs are when they stretch?
The dog pose teaches us to be humble and accept our bodies
as they are. With practice, almost anyone can manage the dog
pose, and as with anything, practice makes progress.

1 Kneel on your bottom with your head on the floor and your arms stretched out in front of you.

2 Push back on your heels and raise your bottom so that you make a triangle.

3 Push your heels down into the floor and make sure your spine is straight.

4 Hold the pose for as long as you can, then lower your bottom back onto your heels, and rest for a while with your head on the floor before you sit up.

If you can't straighten your back, it is a good idea to try this pose with your knees bent.

Chang says his mama's an architect.

Sometimes, my daddy's a triangle.

The Triangle Pose
Trikonasana

Triangles are the most stable of the geometric shapes. The triangle pose teaches us to be strong, to build a foundation of support and to relax under pressure. Triangles have three sides and three angles — just as we have three aspects: mind, body and spirit.

1 Jump your feet apart and stretch out your arms at the same time.

2 Turn your right foot so that its heel points to the middle of your left foot.

3 As you exhale, tilt your upper body from the waist over to the right until your right hand reaches your right ankle. Inhale.

4 Now exhale and turn your head to look up at your left thumb.

5 To come out of the pose, reverse these movements.

6 Repeat on the left side.

Anna says her step-dad's a pilot.

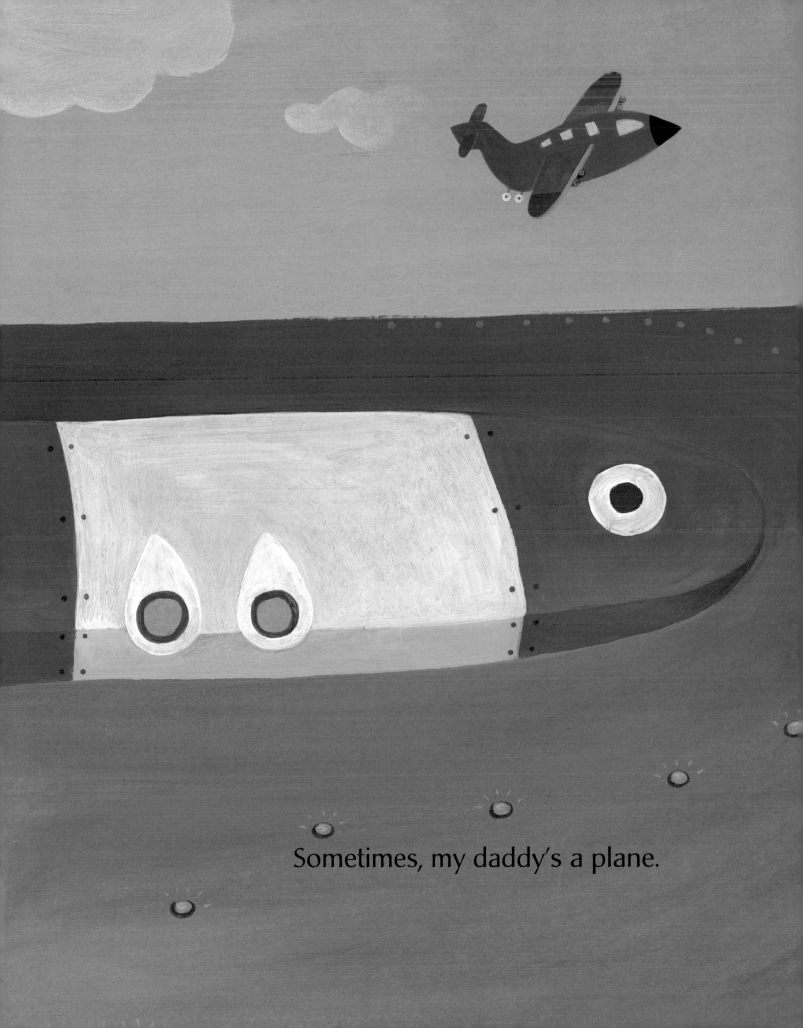

Sometimes, my daddy's a plane.

The Plane Pose
Dekasana

Like a plane that flies high in the sky, this pose teaches us to believe in ourselves so that we can soar through life. Try this posture on both sides and don't worry if you wobble!

1 Stand up straight and raise your right leg so that your thigh is parallel to the floor.

2 Place your hands on your hips and bring your right knee in to your chest.

3 As you exhale, stretch your right leg straight out behind you and swing your upper body down until you are parallel to the floor.

4 Stretch out your arms behind you like wings, palms down.

Malachi says his daddy's a builder.

Sometimes, my daddy's a bridge.

The Bridge Pose
Setu Bandhasana

Ride the changes! Like a bridge that joins one place to another, this pose teaches us to remain strong as we move from one life stage to the next, but also to be flexible, so that we don't break when the winds of change are fierce.

1 Lie on your back with your feet hip-width apart.

2 Slide your heels beneath your knees. As you inhale, tilt your pelvis and lift up your hips until you are on your shoulders.

3 Pull your shoulder blades in and bring your hands together under your back, arms straight.

4 Hold the pose for as long as you are comfortable, then lower your body carefully to the floor.

Emmie says her daddy's a farmer.

Sometimes, my daddy's a plough.

The Plough Pose
Halasana

Like the plough (or plow) that turns the soil over to make
way for new growth, this pose teaches us that overturning
old ways of seeing things sets the ground for inner growth.
If we plough well, we can sow well, and then reap the
rewards of what we have planted.

1 Lie on your back and bring your knees into your chest.

2 As you exhale, raise your legs and hips straight up, rolling onto the back of your shoulders and using your hands to support your back. Inhale.

3 As you exhale, lower your legs down to the floor behind your head.

4 To come out of the pose, reverse these movements.

Sita says her mother's a marine biologist.

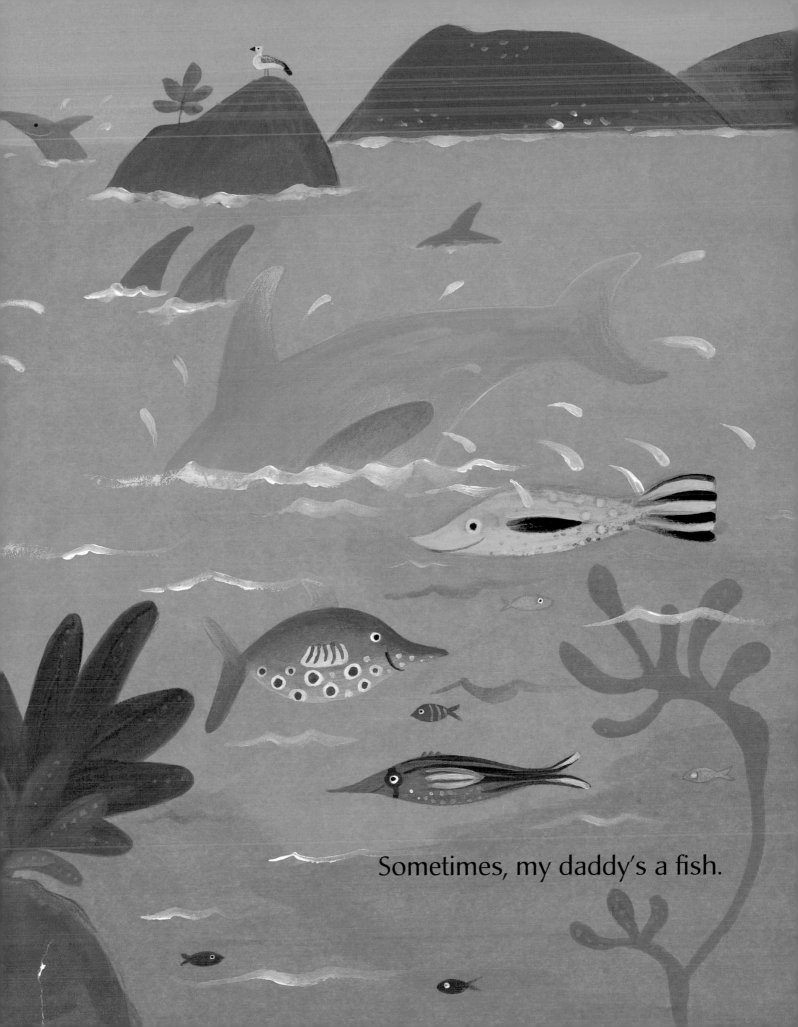

Sometimes, my daddy's a fish.

The Fish Pose
Matsyasana

The fish pose teaches us how to relax and accept the flow
of life that carries and supports us on our journey – don't
struggle upstream, jump in and just go with the flow, even
in turbulent times.

1 Sit on the floor with your legs straight and your hands under your bottom, palms down, toes pointed.

2 Lean back until your forearms are on the floor. Pull your elbows, forearms and shoulder blades close together.

3 As you inhale, arch your back, lower your head and slide back until your crown is resting on the floor.

4 To release the pose, bring your arms back to your sides and slowly uncurve until you are lying flat on the floor.

Pedro says his daddy works in Zambia.

Sometimes, my daddy's a lion.

The Lion Pose
Simhasana

Lions are brave and they have fierce roars! This pose
encourages us to feel and express our power and courage.
It challenges us to be bold, and to overcome our fears.

1 Kneel on the floor with your bottom on your heels.

2 Separate your legs at the knees.

3 Bend down and place your hands in front of you, fingers pointing out.

4 Tuck in your chin, stick your tongue out and roar!

I say my mama's a baker.

And sometimes my daddy's a pretzel!

The Pretzel Pose (Seated Twist)

Marichyasana

The spine is the core of the body and the core of the nervous system. Using the seated twist helps us to release all kinds of tensions. And just as the body benefits, so too does the mind, letting go of unnecessary thoughts and worries, and becoming confident, open and alert.

1 Bend your right knee and slide your right leg under your left leg, tucking your right foot against your left hip.

2 Draw up your left leg and lift your left foot over your right knee, with the toes pointing forward.

3 Exhaling, twist to the left, starting at the base of the spine, and placing your left hand about a foot behind you for support.

4 Slide your right arm under your left thigh or, if you cannot manage this, press your right elbow against your left knee to give you more leverage.

5 Link your hands together behind your back and twist as far as possible to the left, turning your head to look behind you.

6 Repeat the movement on the other side, following the same sequence.

Bridge

Plough

Fish

Lion

Pretzel

Tips for Young Yogis

The only way to discover what yoga is about is to do it. The best thing about it is that you are in charge! You know better than anyone else how far you can reach, how well you can balance, how still you can be. Yoga is about exploring. Here are some guidelines to help you on your yoga journey:

Preparation and Practice

✦ Don't do yoga right after a meal. Wait for a couple of hours before you start your practice.

✦ Try to do your yoga at the same time each day. If this is too difficult, try to develop a regular routine and fit it in at least two or three times a week.

✦ Yoga is best done little and often; this is much better than doing a lot, then doing nothing, then doing a lot a few weeks later. Make a discipline of it.

✦ Wear loose, comfortable clothing and do your yoga in bare feet on a firm mat to give you stability. If you have long hair, tie it back. Remove loose items like necklaces, bracelets and watches before you start.

✦ When you try the postures in this book, follow the sequence in which they are presented. This order of postures will teach you basic body mechanics, alignment and proper posture and increase your ability to focus and concentrate on a given task.

✦ It is good to stretch, but it is not good to hurt yourself. Challenge yourself but go at your own pace. Staying patient in the pose will teach you how to tolerate conflicts or road blocks and how to resolve them creatively and compassionately and find a better place to be.

✦ Rest for a few minutes at the end of your yoga session.

Having the Right Attitude

✦ Respecting your body means respecting what you put into your body.
If you eat good, fresh foods and drink lots of water, you will feel much
more athletic, alert and alive.

✦ Remember that yoga is not a competition — it's a journey and an
adventure. It's not about being better or worse than anyone else, it's
about getting to know yourself better and improving your skills in
the process.

✦ Believe in yourself! If you think you can do it, you will do it. You
may not be successful straight away, but with practice, patience and
persistence, you will grow and grow — the sky's the limit!

✦ Yoga is not just about your body becoming supple and strong and
open. It's about letting your mind and your spirit grow supple and
strong and open too. Watch what is going on in your head and if
there are lots of junky thoughts going round and round, throw them
out — you don't need them. All they are doing is weighing you down!
Your real power can't get in if there is too much junk floating around
inside your head! Develop your ability to observe, identify, accept and
work with your own thoughts and feelings.

✦ It's important to develop a compassionate and conscientious attitude
towards yourself and you'll learn how to deal with inner obstacles
and cultivate confidence, resilience, courage and tolerance in order to
navigate through outer challenges. These valuable qualities are the
benefits of the yoga process and become lifetime tools for vitality.

Yoga and Your Life

✦ Yoga is more than a way of exercising; it's also a way of life. Don't just do the postures; think about what they mean to you and relate them to what's happening in your world.

✦ Yoga can help you get unstuck if you are unhappy about something in your life. Explore the postures and focus on the ones that are most important to you. For example, if there is a lot of change happening in your life, you can build yourself a bridge — in fact, you can be your own bridge. If you are feeling afraid or nervous, you can boost your courage with the lion pose.

✦ The physical demands of yoga teach you how to navigate and negotiate many challenges. Achieving physical strength, alignment, balance, flexibility and integration takes focus, determination and finesse. You can apply these skills to other areas of your life.

✦ If you do yoga with your mother or father, or your schoolteacher, don't fool around but don't be too serious either. Do what you can and have fun.

✦ Bring your yoga skills to the other areas of your life. For instance, at school use your yoga skills of relaxing, focusing and concentrating during a difficult test, or try using more patience, respect and confidence with your friends.

✦ This book is just one step on your yoga journey. If you enjoy it, and you want to know more, find out if there are any yoga classes in your area or ask your schoolteacher to set up a class. Yoga is fun in a group, and you can learn fast if you have a good teacher — just like the children in this story!